Moose
The Goose

And

The Big Day

Gene Goodson

Hi, my name is Moose. My grandpa Tom always calls me Moose the Goose. This is funny because I'm not a moose or a goose.

I'm a dog. I'm a very special dog. I have really curly tan hair that looks like noodles hanging from my body. I have cute brown paws

My eyes were bright sparkling blue when I was a little puppy but have changed to green since I got older.

I love to smile showing my bright white teeth and my long slick pink tongue. I want to tell you all about my big day.

When I was just a little puppy. I was adopted by a new family.

Adopted means I get to move to a new place with new parents.

ADOPTED

I was picked up by my new "hoomans". There was a mommy hooman and three girl hoomans. They loaded me into a car and I got to take a long car ride. I learned that day that I love riding in cars. Cars really go fast, even faster than I can run.

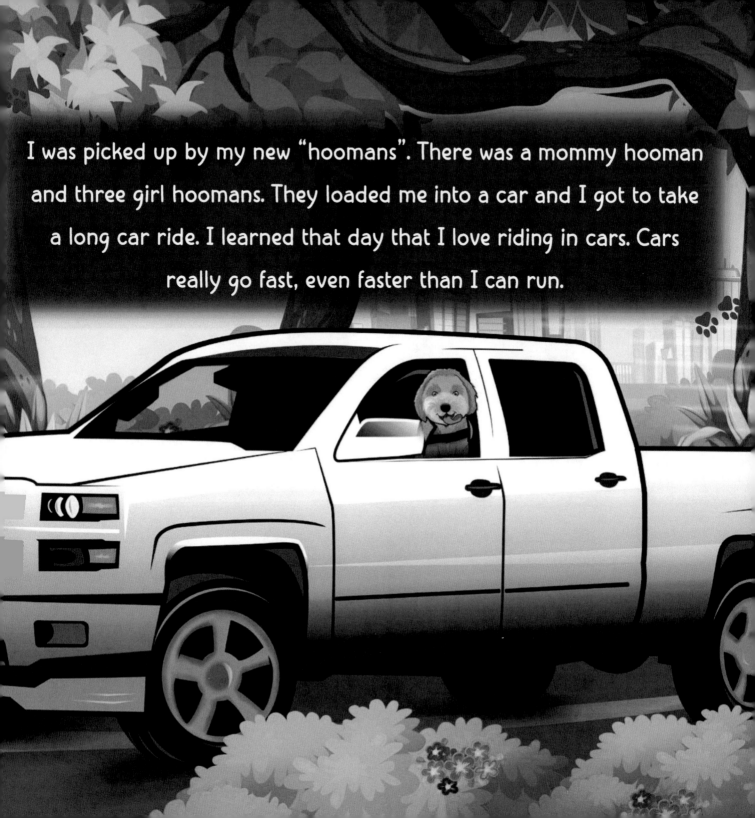

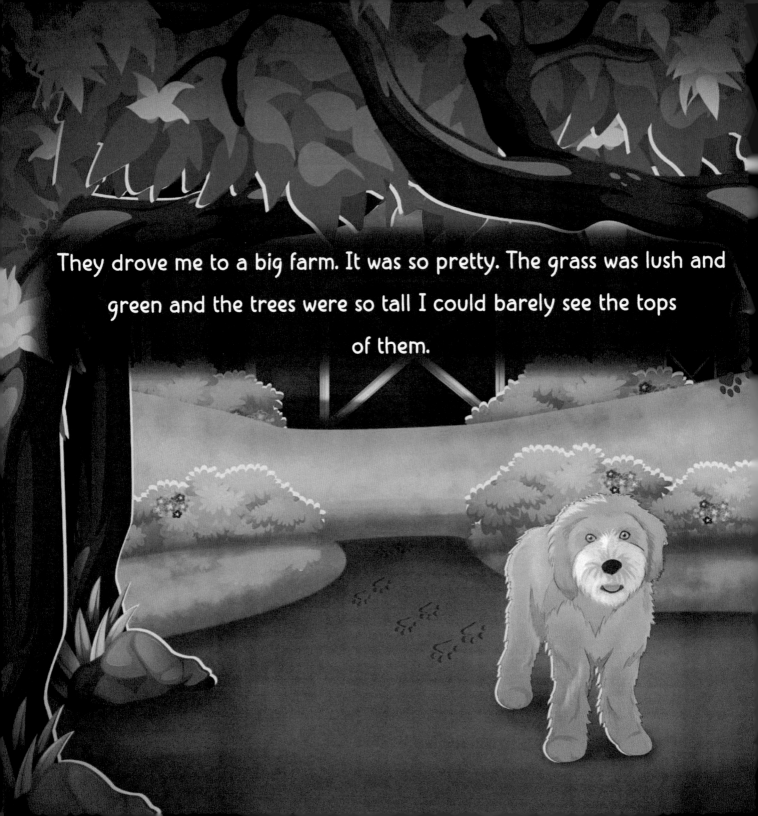

They drove me to a big farm. It was so pretty. The grass was lush and green and the trees were so tall I could barely see the tops of them.

There were a bunch of different smells at the farm and they all smelled like heaven. The dirt was so brown, soft, and rich and it squished between my toes leaving footprints everywhere I walked.

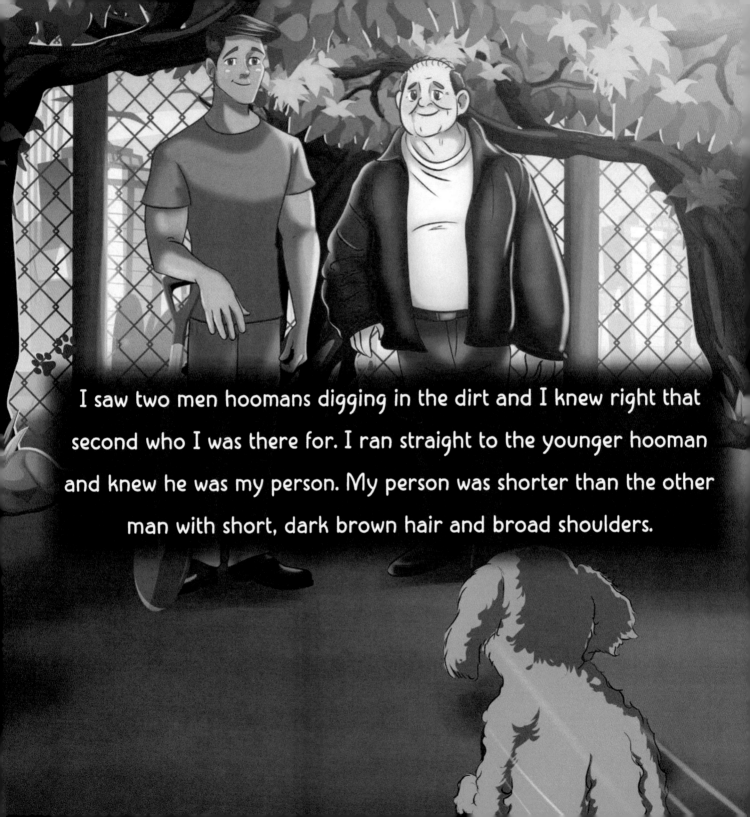

I saw two men hoomans digging in the dirt and I knew right that second who I was there for. I ran straight to the younger hooman and knew he was my person. My person was shorter than the other man with short, dark brown hair and broad shoulders.

His name was Gene but everyone called him dad. I think I'll call him dad too. I could tell he was surprised to see me when he kneeled down to me.

He scooped me up like I was a feather. When he looked into my eyes, his eyes started leaking water. The water from his eyes seemed to be happy water because he kept smiling and kissing my nose.

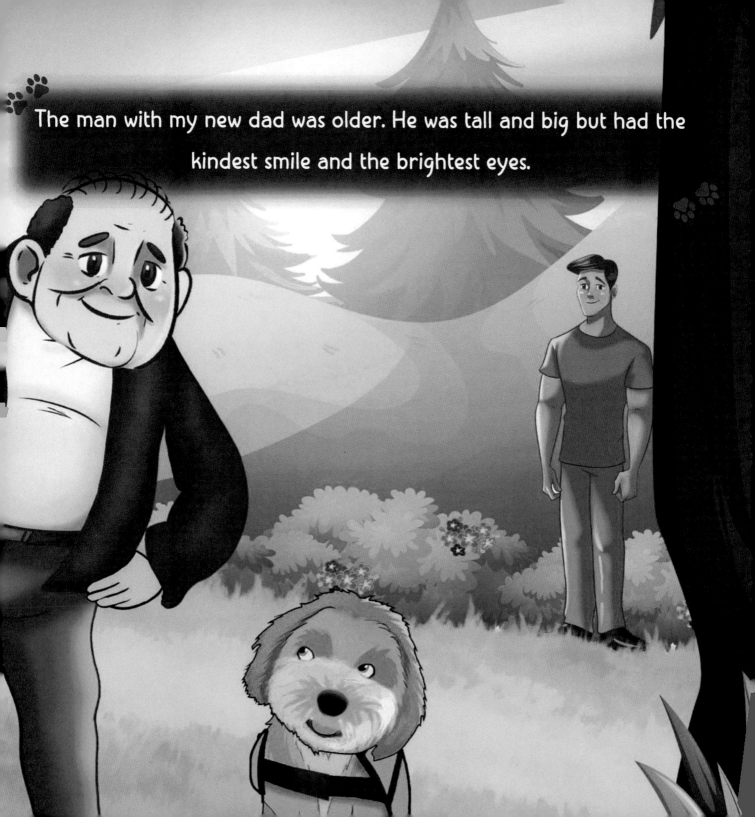

The man with my new dad was older. He was tall and big but had the kindest smile and the brightest eyes.

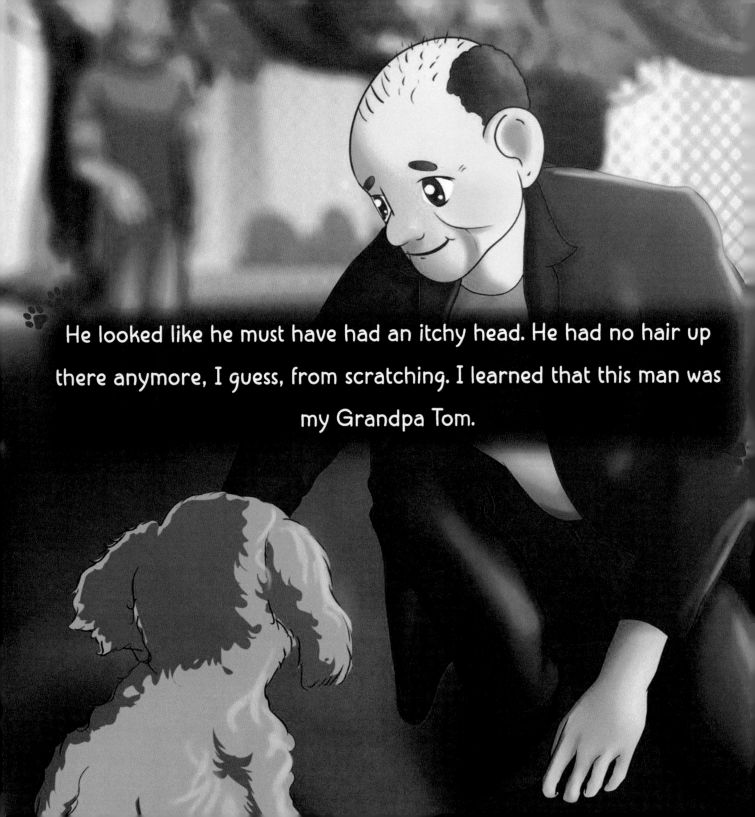

He looked like he must have had an itchy head. He had no hair up there anymore, I guess, from scratching. I learned that this man was my Grandpa Tom.

Everyone gathered around us and the small girls told my new dad that my name was Moose. "Moose the Goose" said grandpa Tom, who was smiling happily.

I loved my new dad and I took him everywhere I went. We spent so much time together. I could tell if my dad was sad, nervous, scared or happy. I didn't know big people got scared too but they do.

When I could tell my dad was feeling bad I would jump up in his lap and kiss and lick all over his face. I was so good at making my dad feel better and I really liked helping him.

He decided to send me to a school where I learned to be a service dog. I didn't know what that meant but it sure sounded important.

I will be a good boy
I will be a good boy
I will be a good boy
I will be a good boy
I will be a good boy
I will be a good boy
I will be a good boy

I was just a few months old and I already had to go to school. I guess when I think about it, I was going to school to learn how to be a superhero.

My dad even got me a special vest to wear. It was bright green and covered my entire back. It had a sign on both sides that said "service dog".

I loved my vest but it was way too big and even dragged the ground when I tried to walk. I sure hope I grow into this thing.

I found out I had a job, and that was helping my dad when he felt bad, and boy was it a big job.

I even had my dad sleep in my big bed with me. He thinks it's his bed but I know the truth. I'll let him think it's his bed for now.

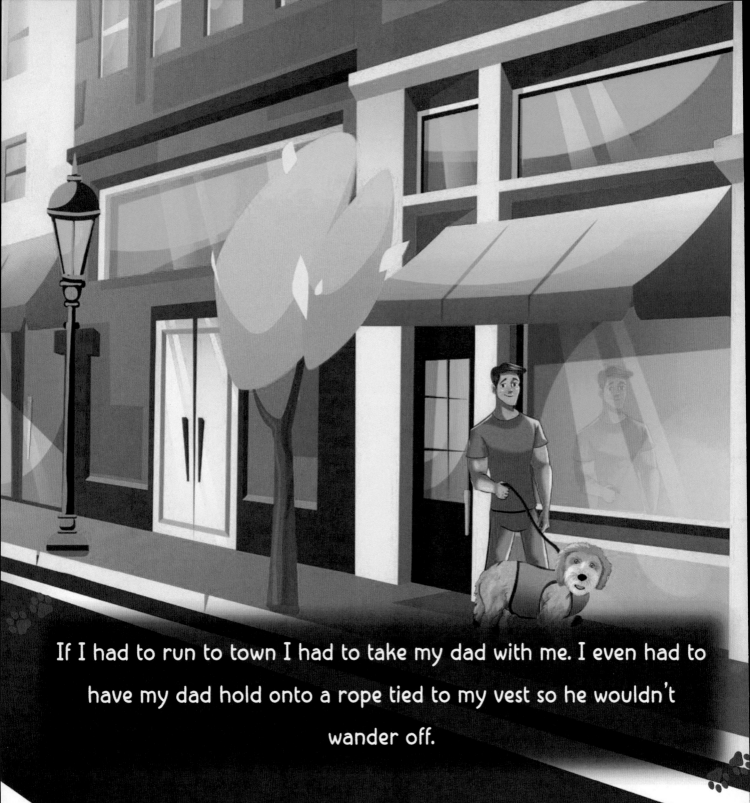

If I had to run to town I had to take my dad with me. I even had to have my dad hold onto a rope tied to my vest so he wouldn't wander off.

I was always working with my dad but it was ok because I loved doing it so much.

I love my job and understand how important it is. When I wear my vest I can't talk to other people because I have to watch my person.

When I got to take my vest off I could run and jump and play just like other dogs. But remember if you see me out and about with my vest walking my person, don't talk to me or try to pet me. I'm busy with work and can't play.

So that's my big day. I learned a lot. I got a new family and a job that is so much fun. I know this is the start of many exciting adventures with my dad.

This is Moose the Goose saying I'll see you all soon.

 Gene Goodson spent his adult life as a State Trooper for the great state of Oklahoma, retiring after 22 years of service. Seeing a need in society for positive male role models, he created a volunteer group of men known as "Fathers Are In The House" or simply F.A.I.T.H. the group would greet the children in the mornings at the schools and read books to them in the classroom. This sparked Gene's interest in writing stories about his service dog Moose to educate and entertain children of all ages.

Gene and his best friend Moose live in Northwest Oklahoma with his wife and daughters. Their real life adventures together spark the true tales of the Moose the Goose stories.

Made in the USA
Coppell, TX
13 December 2024

42444367R00021